W9-CMT-840

The Berenstain Bears and the TROUBLE WITH COMMERCIALS

TV commercials
are entertaining, indeed.
But they also can make you
buy stuff you don't need.

The Berenstain Bears and the TROUBLE WITH COMMERCIALS

Stan & Jan Berenstain
with Mike Berenstain

HarperFestival®
A Division of HarperCollins*Publishers*

The Berenstain Bears and the Trouble with Commercials
 For information address HarperCollins Children's Books, a division of HarperCollins Publishers, 1350 Avenue of the Americas, New York, NY 10019.
www.harpercollinschildrens.com
Library of Congress catalog card number: 2006928096
ISBN-10: 0-06-057403-8 (trade bdg.) — ISBN-13: 978-0-06-057403-1 (trade bdg.)
ISBN-10: 0-06-057387-2 (pbk.) — ISBN-13: 978-0-06-057387-4 (pbk.)
❖
First Edition

Every day after school, Brother Bear and Sister Bear took a TV break before they started their homework. They got some milk and cookies, settled down in front of the TV, and watched their favorite shows.

Sometimes it was *The Bear Stooges* or *Doofus Duck*.

Sometimes it was *Rabid Rabbits* or *Wacky Wart Hog*.

But whatever it was, there was one thing that they always looked forward to—the commercials!

Some of the commercials were better than the shows. They had better music, better jokes, better singing and dancing—they were fun!

And because they were so much fun, Brother and Sister always wound up wanting what the commercials were selling. It didn't matter what it was—cereal or candy or toys or a trip to Grizzyland—that's what they had to have.

"Now, Brother and Sister," sighed Mama Bear after the cubs had asked for one more super-delicious honey-sweetened breakfast treat, "you haven't even finished that big box of cereal you asked for just a few days ago!"

"But this cereal is extra super-special!" insisted the cubs. "Happy Hamster, the Super Cereal spokes-rodent said so!"

"I don't care if Doofus Duck himself says so!" said Mama. "I'm not buying you one more thing you saw on a commercial!"

But a few days later, Brother and Sister were eating their extra super-special cereal. They had pleaded and pestered Mama so much that she couldn't stand it. She had given in and bought it. The old box of cereal that the cubs hadn't even finished went into the trash.

SUPER
CEREAL
Yummies

Mama grew so fed up with the cubs asking for the things they saw on commercials that she decided it was time to pull the plug on the TV.

The problem was that she and Papa had favorite shows, too, and they would miss them. Mama usually watched *Ms. Clara's Garden Show* every morning and Papa watched *Fishing with Uncle Finn* in the evening. Not only that, the cubs watched TV at their friends' houses and came home begging for things they saw in commercials there, too.

FRED

Mama was at her wit's end. "Brother and Sister just don't seem to understand," she complained to Papa one day when she was watering her houseplants. "They don't understand that you can't buy everything you see in a commercial. Why, if you did that, you'd wind up with a houseful of expensive things you don't really need!"

Papa noticed that Mama was using the special limited edition Ms. Clara watering can she had bought after seeing a commercial for it on *Ms. Clara's Garden Show*.

"I see what you mean," he said thoughtfully. "Maybe I should talk to them about that."

Ms. Clara

So Papa talked to Brother and Sister. He explained that TV commercials were just there to sell things. He explained that commercials sometimes exaggerated a little. “You can’t buy something every time somebody tells you to,” he said. “You’ve got to be smart shoppers. You’ve got to pick and choose or you’ll wind up with a lot of things you don’t really need. You two understand that, don’t you?”

“Oh yes, Papa,” said Brother and Sister. “We understand!”

But they didn't. They went right back to asking for every Bearbie Doll, Space Grizzly Action Figure, and Big Bag of Honey-Gummy-Wummy Bears they saw on TV.

"We need a plan!" Papa said to Mama. They put their heads together and thought and thought and came up with a plan.

The cereal, toy, and candy companies always saved their best commercials for Saturday morning. So the next Saturday morning when the cubs came begging for things they saw on TV, Mama put the plan to work.

This time, the great new cereal that they just *had* to have was Rainbow Swirl Bits. The toys were Banana Invaders from Outer Space and Lovey Dovey Dolls. And the candy was Super-Duper Sour Suckers.

Mama sat the cubs down on the sofa away from the TV and said, "Now, listen carefully."

"We're listening," said the cubs.

"We've tried to explain to you that you can't possibly have everything you see on TV."

"Yes, Mama," said the cubs.

“So, here’s what we’re going to do,” said Mama. “We’re going to buy all these things you’re so excited about: the cereal, the toys, the candy.”

“Yippee!” cried the cubs.

"*But*, and it's a big but," said Mama, "you have to promise not ever to mention another commercial until you've eaten every single Rainbow Swirl Bit, every single Super-Duper Sour Sucker, and played with the Banana Invaders from Outer Space and Lovey Dovey Dolls for a whole month. Do you promise?"

“We promise! We promise!” cried the cubs.

As it turned out, the cubs didn't like Rainbow Swirl Bits very much.

"Yuck!" said Brother. "They turn the milk purple!"

"And then they turn to purple mush!" said Sister.

But a promise is a promise.

The Banana Invaders from Outer Space weren't much fun either. They were just plastic bananas with rocket guns, and there wasn't much you could do with them.

And the Lovey Dovey Dolls had hair that you were supposed to comb, but it all came out.

And the Super-Duper Sour Suckers were so sour the cubs' mouths puckered up so badly that they could hardly speak.

But a promise was a promise.

Mama and Papa's plan worked. The cubs not only kept their promise, they learned not to get too excited about the things they saw on commercials.

But as it happened, not *everybody* learned the lesson. One evening Papa was watching his favorite show, *Fishing with Uncle Finn*, when a commercial came on. It was for Uncle Finn's Guaranteed Magic Light Fishing Lure.

"Did you see that?" cried Papa. "It lights up and is guaranteed to catch fish!"

"But Papa," said Brother, "how do you know it will do all those things?"

"Well, gee," said Papa. "Do you think Uncle Finn would lie?"

"No," said Sister. "But he might just exaggerate a little."

MAGIC LIGHT

"Hmm," said Papa. He liked Uncle Finn a lot and watched the rest of the show. But he had second thoughts about buying Uncle Finn's Guaranteed Magic Light Fishing Lure.